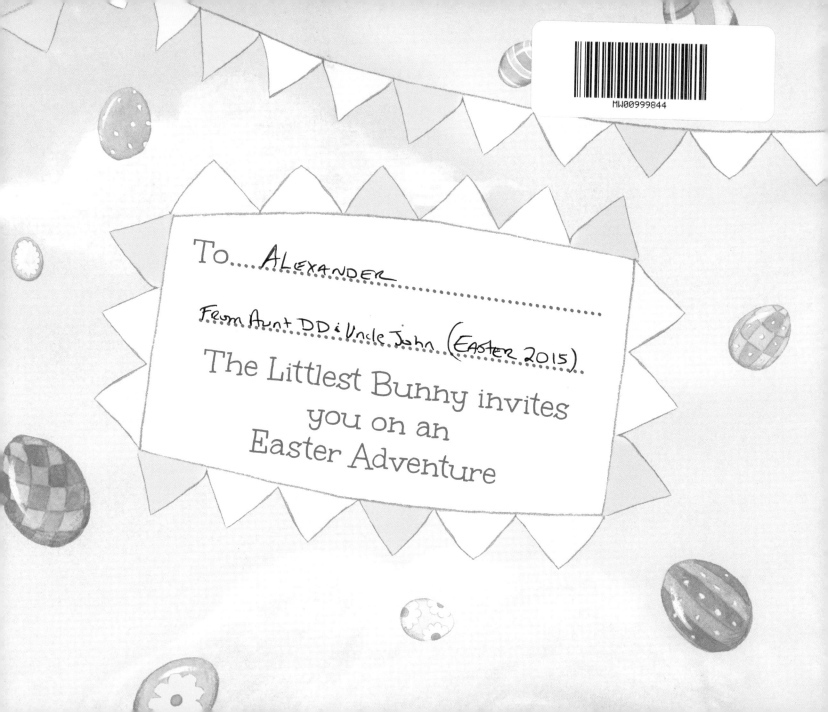

To....ALEXANDER............................
....

From Aunt DD & Uncle John (Easter 2015).

The Littlest Bunny invites
you on an
Easter Adventure

MW00999844

an Easter Adventure

The Littlest Bunny in New Jersey

MAY

JOE

Written by Lily Jacobs
Illustrated by Robert Dunn and Katherine Kirkland
Designed by Sarah Allen

Text copyright © 2015 by Sourcebooks, Inc.
Design and cover copyright © Hometown World Ltd. and Sourcebooks, Inc.

Sourcebooks and the colophon are registered trademarks of Sourcebooks, Inc.
All rights reserved. No part of this book may be reproduced in any form or by any electronic or mechanical means including information storage and retrieval
systems–except in the case of brief quotations embodied in critical articles or reviews–without permission in writing from its publisher, Sourcebooks, Inc.

The characters and events portrayed in this book are fictitious or are used fictitiously. Any similarity to real persons, living or dead, is purely coincidental and
not intended by the author.

Published by Sourcebooks Jabberwocky, an imprint of Sourcebooks, Inc.
P.O. Box 4410, Naperville, Illinois 60567-4410
(630) 961-3900
Fax: (630) 961-2168
www.jabberwockykids.com

Library of Congress Cataloging-in-Publication data is on file with the publisher.

Source of Production: Leo Paper Products, Guangdong Province, China
Date of Production: September 2014
Run Number: HTW_PO250714
Printed and bound in China
10 9 8 7 6 5 4 3 2 1

an Easter Adventure

The Littlest Bunny in New Jersey

Written by Lily Jacobs
Illustrated by Robert Dunn

sourcebooks
jabberwocky

Not long ago, in a land you might know,
Lived a girl named May and a boy named Joe.

WELCOME TO NEW JERSEY

They had moved to New Jersey, and longed to explore.
Make new friends, have adventures, and many things more!

New Jersey
BUNNY

New Jersey Pet Store

On the day before Easter,
they rode into town.
They went to the pet store
and looked all around.

There in the front
was a pen full of bunnies.
The small ones were cute,
and the big ones were funny.

They played with the bunnies
and thought for a bit,
And then they agreed
on the most *perfect* fit:

The *littlest* bunny,
with the sweetest small hop.

"He's ours!" May announced.
"Let's call him Flop."

So Flop joined the family
that sunny spring day.
The littlest bunny
was now home to stay.

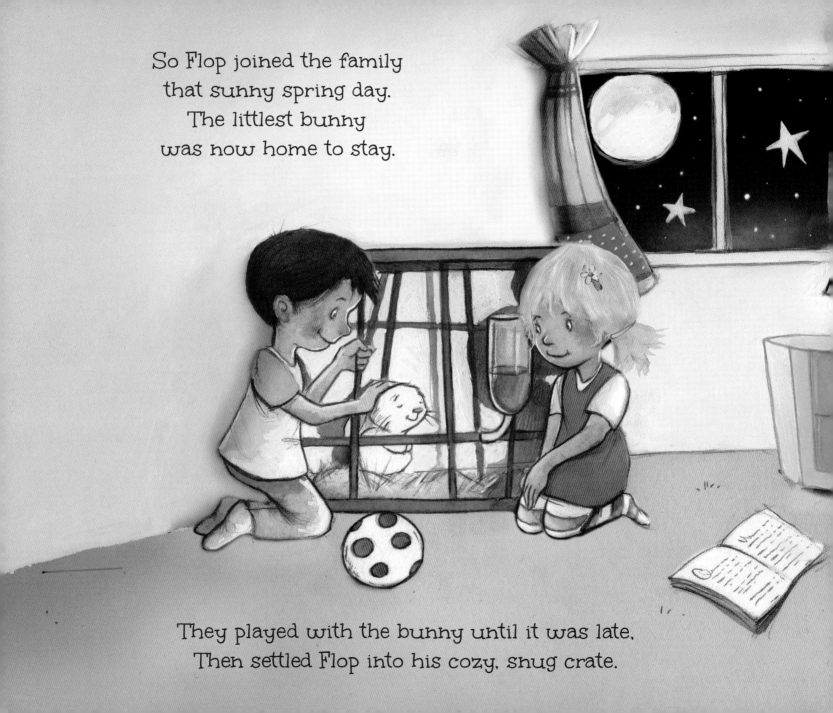

They played with the bunny until it was late,
Then settled Flop into his cozy, snug crate.

May gave Flop a kiss
and Joe patted his head,
And then the two children
both climbed into bed.

A soft evening breeze blew in through the window,
And May and Joe smiled as they slept on their pillows.

But Flop had no time now
to close his own eyes:
He was preparing
an Easter surprise!

He was quite little,
that much was true,
But tonight our dear Flop
had a big job to do.

For he had a secret
he hadn't let show:

He was the Easter Bunny, and he had to go!

A magical wind gave his whiskers a tickle.
His nose, how it twitched! His ears, how they wiggled!

Soon, Flop was quite different than ever before.
And he couldn't wait—not for one moment more!

He raced through the house and out into the night,
To where he had hidden his eggs out of sight.

Map of New Jersey

His marvelous burrow held Easter eggs plenty:
To be quite exact, **nine million and twenty!**
He packed up the eggs; he looked at the map.
He fastened his goggles and his red flying cap.

Then Flop hopped right into
his hot air balloon,
And soon he was soaring
as high as the moon!

As he watched his first stop grow nearer and nearer, His **Garden State mission** became even clearer.

First, Flop balanced eggs
on a tall building top...

DORBROOK
PARK

...Then he went to
the park, spreading
eggs as he hopped.

And then he dashed off
for an Easter home run...

...Then quietly hid
chocolate eggs, one by one.

With big bounces here and giant jumps there,

Flop hid New Jersey's eggs everywhere!

WEST   EAST

He flew to the **east**, to the **south**, **west**, and **north**. He crisscrossed the state; he raced **back** and **forth**.

Hoboken, Newark, and Ridgewood got treats.
Then Westfield, Jersey City, and Wayne were complete.

Cherry Hill and Toms River—the long list went on.
Flop was delivering his eggs until dawn!

Finally, Flop found his very last stop.
He came to *your* house with a bounce and a hop!
And there he delivered his Easter surprises:
So many eggs, of all shapes and sizes!
And when he was done,
he stopped for a rest.

Yes, surely this Easter
was one of his best!

The morning sun rose on that bright Easter day.
It was time to wake up for Joe and for May.
But when they went over to find their friend Flop,

The door was wide open—
his crate was unlocked!

There were eggs to discover, as all children know.
"But we just want Flop!" cried May and cried Joe.

They looked under their beds; they looked all around.
But the littlest bunny just couldn't be found.

But whose goggles were these?

Who unfolded this map?

Then from 'round the corner came a faint *tap-tap-tap.*
They rushed and they stumbled. It had to be him!
And there they found baskets—
and something else was tucked in?

"It's Flop!" they cried out, and held him so close.
Joe tickled his ears and May kissed his pink nose.
Flop hugged them back, his new friends so dear.

Happy Easter, New Jersey!
See you next year!

Did you find all the Easter eggs
hidden in New Jersey?
Look back through the book to see
if you can spot all 20 eggs.

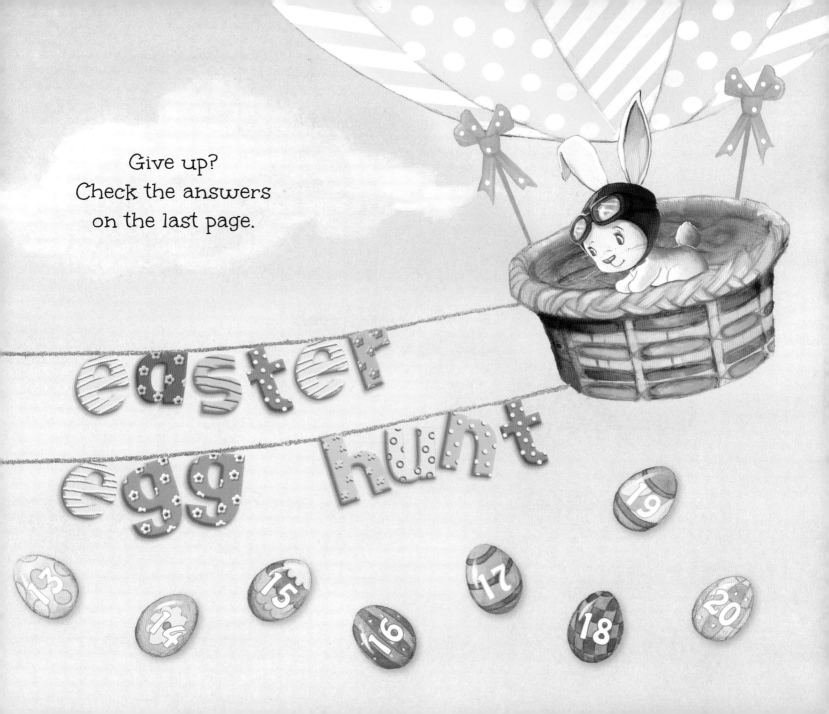

Give up?
Check the answers
on the last page.

easter
egg hunt